An Elephant's Standing in There

Written by Scott Pratt
and
Illustrated by Kody Storm Rowe

An Elephant's Standing in There

The first time I saw him I tried
   not to run,
'Cause I'm not a sissy, I swear,
But what else do you do when
   you walk in your room,

AND AN ELEPHANT'S STANDING IN THERE?

I wasn't about to give
him the chance,
To eat me or step
on my head,

I dashed down the
hallway and on
through the house,
And jumped in my
Mom and Dad's bed.

I squeezed in between them and
closed my eyes tight,
But Dad wouldn't have it, he said:
"Get up little buddy, go back to
your room,
Go back there and get in your bed."

"I can't, Dad," I
    whispered, "Don't
    make me go back.
I can't. No I won't.
    It's not fair.
I can't even get to
    the bed where
    I sleep,
With that elephant
    standing in there!"

"An elephant! What do you mean?" Dad did say.
"The kind with a trunk and big ears?
Well let's just go in there and take us a look,
'Cause I haven't seen one in years."

"Wait, I'll go too," said my
    Mom from the dark,
"It's been a long time for me,
    too.
I haven't laid eyes on an
    elephant's ears,
Since that time we took Joe
    to the zoo."

So off to my bedroom the three of us
   went,
We sneaked as I stifled a yawn,
But wouldn't you know it? We
   got to my room,

AND THAT FLOPPYEARED BUGGER WAS GONE!

"He was here," I protested, "I know that he was.
He looked me right square in the eye.
I thought he might eat me or step on my head,
I swear I did! I wouldn't lie."

"We know that you wouldn't," my
    Mom and Dad said,
As they tucked me back in for the
    night,
"And if he comes back to your room
    before morning,
Just reach up and flip on the

LIGHT."

And sure enough! Just as I
   thought! When they left,
The elephant came to my door.
He stuck his head in with his
   trunk just a-swinging,
He started to walk 'cross the
   floor.

I wanted to yell. I wanted to
   run.
I wanted to crawl through the
   wall.
But I couldn't speak and I sure
   couldn't move.
I just couldn't do nothin' at all.

Just then I remembered what Mom and Dad said,
And I reached out to turn on the light,
But that elephant's trunk wrapped around my
   small arm,
And I thought I might die from the fright.

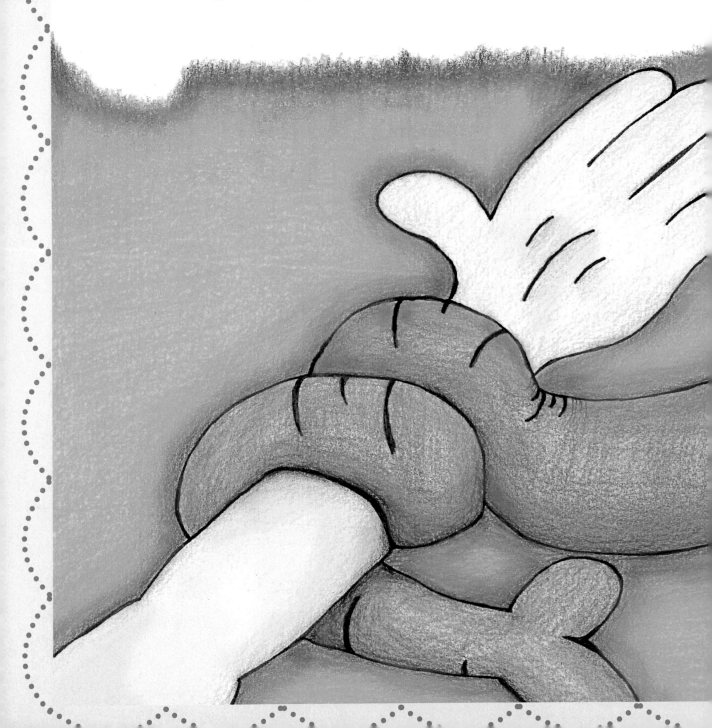

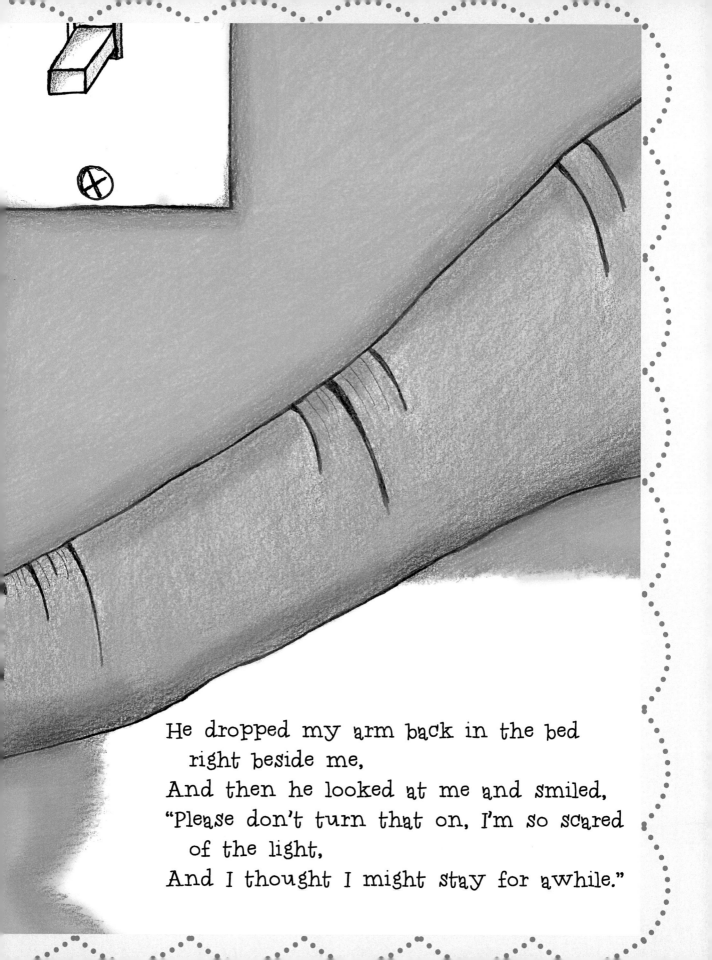

He dropped my arm back in the bed
   right beside me,
And then he looked at me and smiled,
"Please don't turn that on, I'm so scared
   of the light,
And I thought I might stay for awhile."

The elephant said that he sure wouldn't hurt me,
He wouldn't hurt nuthin', he said.

He just wanted someone to lie down
beside of,
Could he lie on the floor by my bed?

I told him he could so he did and we talked,
We talked until it was near dawn,

And when Momma came in and woke me
for breakfast,

My floppyeared friend, he was gone.

He comes back to see me sometimes in
    the night,
He comes when I most want him to,
We talk about jungles and things that
    he knows,
We talk about things I know, too.

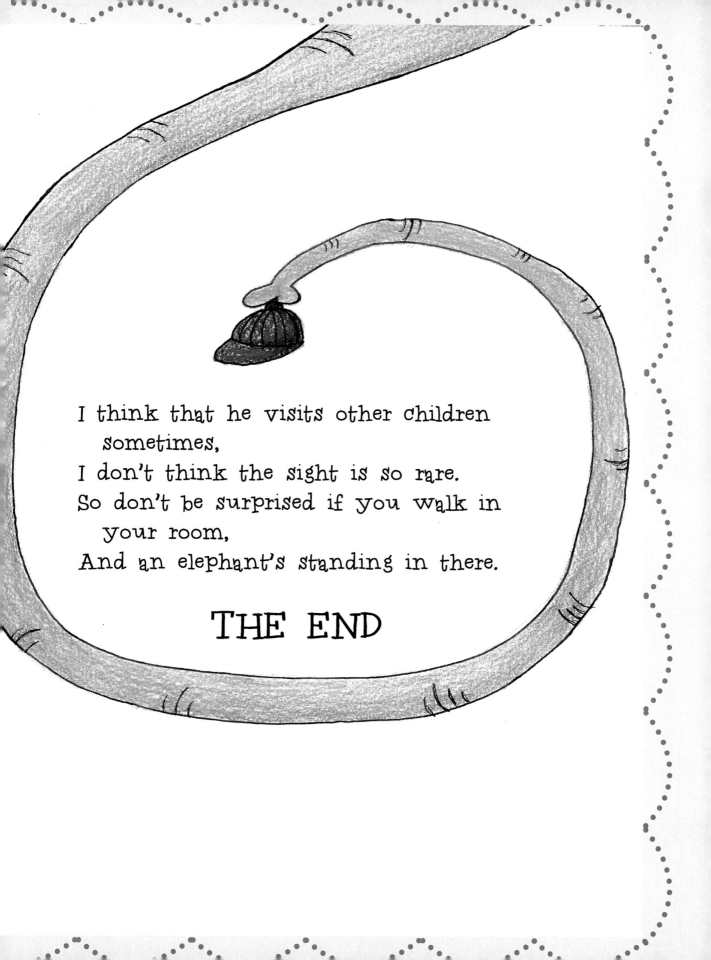

I think that he visits other children
    sometimes,
I don't think the sight is so rare.
So don't be surprised if you walk in
    your room,
And an elephant's standing in there.

THE END

Made in the USA
San Bernardino, CA
23 March 2019